Marcel the Shell With Shoes On: Things About Me

RAZORBILL

Published by the Penguin Group
Penguin Young Readers Group
345 Hudson Street, New York, New York 10014, U.S.A.
Penguin Group (USA) Inc., 375 Hudson Street, New York, New York 10014, U.S.A.
Penguin Group (Canada), 90 Eglinton Avenue East, Suite 700, Toronto, Ontario, Canada M4P 2Y3
(a division of Pearson Penguin Canada Inc.)
Penguin Books Ltd, 80 Strand, London WC2R 0RL, England
Penguin Ireland, 25 St Stephen's Green, Dublin 2, Ireland (a division of Penguin Books Ltd)
Penguin Group (Australia), 250 Camberwell Road, Camberwell, Victoria 3124, Australia
(a division of Pearson Australia Group Pty Ltd)
Penguin Books India Pvt Ltd, 11 Community Centre, Panchsheel Park, New Delhi – 110 017, India
Penguin Group (NZ), 67 Apollo Drive, Mairangi Bay, Auckland 1311, New Zealand
(a division of Pearson New Zealand Ltd)
Penguin Books (South Africa) (Pty) Ltd, 24 Sturdee Avenue, Rosebank, Johannesburg 2196, South Africa

Penguin Books Ltd, Registered Offices: 80 Strand, London WC2R 0RL, England

10 9 8

ISBN 978-1-59514-455-3

Library of Congress Cataloging-in-Publication Data is available

Printed in China

Marcel the Shell

with Shoes On

Things About Me

By Jenny Slate & Dean Fleischer-Camp

Paintings by Amy Lind

razorbill

An Imprint of Penguin Group (USA) Inc.

Dedicated to our families,

and to each other.

The paintings were painted by Amy Lind, an obviously brilliant artist, in her new home in Savannah, GA. They are based on photographs shot by David A. Erickson, a great talent and friend, in Brooklyn, N.Y., in collaboration with Dean Fleischer-Camp, who also did all of the lettering & drawings.

My name is Marcel and I'm Partially a Shell, as you Can See on my body. But I also have shoes...

...and...

... a Face!

I like that about myself and I like myself, and I have a lot of other great qualities as well.

This is my Breadroom.

It's a Bedroom. But I sleep in a piece of Bread. So I just Call it my Breadroom.

I love where I live.
I have a lot of really
interesting neighbors.

We are known
for our famous
Monuments.

I often visit the Aquarium
It's the only place
where you're allowed
to stare.

Sometimes you really do need to get a good look at things.

We also have an Amusement Park.

Guess which ride I'm too afraid to go on?

the Salad Spinner

I don't need a thrill ride.

I'm already thrilled enough.

Guess which ride I love?

The Ladle!

Guess how I dry off?

My one regret in life

is that I'll never have a dog.

His name is Alan.

He doesn't Know any
tricks or anything.

Tell him to roll Over...

See?

One time I sniffed a fleck of pepper and I sneezed so hard I sneezed a hundred times a day for a month.

Guess what I use as a helmet?

A Pistachio

Guess what I need a helmet for?

— Because once or twice a year I climb the Sandal.

Some people say that my head is too big for my body and then I say...

On Saturdays I like to go
See a movie with my Grandmother.

I even treat myself to a large popCorn.

Sometimes at night I like to write down a
list of everything I did that day.

...But I get so exhausted from
lifting the pencil that I
usually just call it a night.

Could you tell
me what time
it is?

Could you shut the Book please ?

I'm trying to go to Bread.

...Compared to

What?

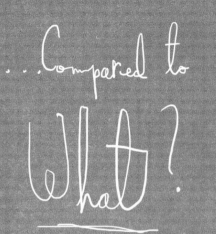